AJ's
Mystery

AJ's Mystery

Karla Erickson

Illustrated by
Sandy F. Gagon

Bookcraft
Salt Lake City, Utah

Library of Congress Catalog Card Number: 95–60341

ISBN 0–88494–983–4

First Printing, 1995

Printed in the United States of America

To Kelli, Kacee, and Kristy—
the inspiration for the AJ series

Contents

1

The White Van

What's that white van doing in our neighborhood? AJ wondered as she watched the vehicle circle the block for the second time. There were no back windows, and the front windows were tinted so dark that AJ couldn't tell who was driving the van. *Why is it going so slow?* she wondered.

At that moment, Miranda jumped on AJ, nearly knocking her to the ground. "Miranda!" AJ exclaimed. "You've got to learn not to jump up on people."

AJ sat on the grass, hugging the lovable dog. "You know I can't get mad at you, don't you," AJ said, running her fingers through Miranda's thick golden fur. Although the golden retriever was her grandmother's dog, AJ loved her as her own.

Miranda stiffened and growled a deep, throaty growl. She was looking at the white van, which had stopped in front of AJ's yard. AJ's heart quickened. She grabbed Miranda's collar.

"C'mon, girl," she said quietly, "let's go in the backyard."

AJ glanced around as the van started moving slowly. As soon as she had locked Miranda inside her pen, she raced into the kitchen. Her grandmother was standing at the sink.

"Grandma," AJ gasped, "there's a strange van outside. It keeps driving around our neighborhood, and it stopped right in front of our house."

Grandmother quickly wiped her hands on a towel. "Let's get the license plate number," she said, hurrying toward the front door.

But they were too late. As they opened the door, the white van disappeared around the corner.

"I wonder why they keep driving around here," said AJ. "I had a real scared feeling when I saw them stop in front of our house. Do you think they're robbers or something?"

Grandmother sat down on the sofa. "No, I don't think they're robbers. Maybe they're lost and looking for someone's house number," she suggested, not wanting to frighten AJ.

AJ looked at her grandmother sitting on the couch. She seemed so pale and tired. "Grandma, are you okay?" AJ asked, sitting down beside her.

Grandma took her hand and managed a smile. "I'm fine, AJ. I'm just a little tired, that's all."

Ever since Grandma had come to live with AJ's family, it seemed she was always tired. *Maybe it's because she's getting older,* thought AJ. "Are you sure you're not sick?" she asked.

"No, really, AJ," Grandma replied. "I didn't sleep very well last night and I'm afraid it's caught up with me."

At that moment, AJ's mother drove into the driveway. "Looks like Mom picked up Sara at school," said AJ. "I'm glad she did. I don't think Sara should walk home from school with that van around here."

AJ waved. "Hi, Mom."

"Hi, AJ," her mother said cheerfully when she spotted them on the couch. "What are you two so serious about?"

AJ explained about the white van and how they had tried to get the license number.

"That was smart thinking," her mother said. "Too bad you didn't get it. But they probably mean no harm. Maybe they were lost."

"That's what Grandma said," AJ replied. "But I sure had a terrible feeling when it stopped by our home. Even Miranda growled. You know she doesn't growl at anyone."

"If it comes around again, be sure and get the number," said her mother. "Then we can have it checked out by the police."

Six-year-old Sara bounced into the room. "AJ!" she exclaimed. "Look at this picture I drew at school."

AJ couldn't help but show interest. Her little sister was always so cheerful and happy.

"Sara, I think you're going to be an artist," said AJ. "This is really good. I'll bet you're the smartest kid in kindergarten."

Sara beamed.

"AJ, could you take care of Sara while I drive Grandma to the doctor?" her mother asked.

"Oh, my," said Grandma. "I'd forgotten all about that appointment. I'd better hurry and get ready."

"Sure," said AJ. "We'll go outside and play with Miranda. Okay, Sara?"

"Maybe I can draw a picture of Miranda," said her little sister, her big brown eyes sparkling.

"That's a great idea," said AJ. But her thoughts weren't totally on Sara's picture. She couldn't help wondering why her grandmother had been going to the doctor so often.

"AJ," her mother called, "Jen is at a cheerleading practice at school. She'll be late coming home. Jake and Josh will be late, too, because of baseball. Are you sure you can stay with Sara the whole time?"

AJ walked out to the car with her mother and her grandmother. "Don't worry," AJ assured her mother. "I don't have anything else to do. Sara and I are going to play with Miranda. Maybe we can teach her a new trick for obedience school."

As Grandma eased into the car, AJ looked into her eyes. She wanted to ask her if she was sure there was nothing wrong. Instead, she gave her a kiss on the cheek.

"See you in a little while," AJ said.

"We won't be too long," said Grandma.

As they drove away, AJ stood in the driveway. Her thoughts drifted back to the time a few months ago when Grandma came to live with them. She nearly laughed aloud when she recalled the two of them going to buy flowers for Brother Gruen, her neighbor. What fun she and Grandma had together. Even when Grandma slammed on the brakes to miss a dog and the flowers had fallen all over the floor, Grandma made sure it all turned out okay. She was like that.

"I sure love her," AJ whispered.

"Who do you love?" asked Sara. AJ hadn't noticed Sara come outside.

"I was thinking how much I love Grandma," said AJ.

"I do too," said Sara. "I think she's the neatest grandma in the whole world."

AJ couldn't argue with that. But she also knew that the feelings she felt for her grandmother were different from Sara's. AJ's feelings went deeper— deeper than even AJ understood.

"Let's get Miranda," Sara called, interrupting AJ's thoughts.

The sisters raced to the backyard. Of course, Sara won. Miranda wagged her tail when AJ opened the gate to let her out of her pen.

"She misses us when we're at school," said Sara, hugging the furry dog. "She gets bored being in her pen."

"I'm sure you're right," said AJ. She tossed a small rubber ball to Sara. "Throw this up into the air and Miranda will jump up and get it."

Sara squealed with delight when Miranda leaped after the ball. Again and again, Sara threw the ball as high as she could.

"Can she fetch?" Sara asked.

"Here's a stick," said AJ. "Miranda's a great fetcher."

Sara threw the stick out into the front yard. Miranda raced after it. When she brought it back to Sara, she was panting hard and wagging her tail.

"Go get this one!" exclaimed Sara. The stick flew through the air.

"No, Sara!" cried AJ. "Don't throw it out into the street."

AJ was too late. Miranda raced after the stick, which now lay in the middle of the road. Sara put her hands over her eyes when she saw a car coming toward Miranda.

"Miranda!" AJ screamed. The sound of screeching brakes caused AJ's heart to pound with fear. As she reached the curb, she breathed a sigh of relief. Miranda stood in the middle of the road with the stick in her mouth. The vehicle had stopped in time. AJ hurried to get her out of the street. As she grabbed the collar, she glanced up to see the vehicle that had nearly hit Miranda. She stared at a white van with dark tinted windows. Fear gripped her. The white van!

"C'mon, Miranda," AJ commanded, her voice shaking.

As soon as they both were on the curb, AJ turned toward the white van. She struggled to see the driver but could only make out the silhouette of what she thought was a man. Slowly, the van started moving. AJ remembered what Grandma said. She must get the license plate number. Her heart was still pounding. She had to remember the number. But when she saw the license plate, she froze. It was an out-of-state plate covered with mud, and AJ couldn't figure out where it was from.

The driver must have sensed that AJ was reading his license plate, because suddenly the engine roared and the white van tore off down the street.

AJ was still shaking as she led Miranda toward her house.

"What's wrong?" Sara asked. "You look scared, AJ."

AJ didn't want to frighten Sara. "I was afraid that Miranda was going to be hit," said AJ. "C'mon, let's take her in the backyard."

AJ's mind was racing. It could be no coincidence that she had spotted the white van so many times in her neighborhood. It must be there for a reason. AJ looked at her cute little sister.

That's it, AJ thought. Why hadn't she thought of this earlier? *They're probably kidnappers and they've seen Sara. They want to kidnap her!*

2

AJ's Suspicions

AJ's heart raced with fear. "Let's go in the house, Sara. I don't feel like playing outside anymore."

Sara told Miranda good-bye as she and AJ closed the door to the pen. As the sisters walked into the house, Sara asked, "Can we put some puzzles together?"

"Sure," said AJ, trying to calm herself. "You pick out the ones you want. While you're doing that, I'm going to call Emily."

AJ waited impatiently, hoping Emily would answer the phone. At last she heard her best friend's voice.

"Em," she said, trying to keep her voice low. "I'm so glad you're home."

"What's wrong?" Emily asked. "You sound as scared as you were the night Benj chased us home after the movie. And why are you talking so quietly?"

"I have to be quiet so Sara can't hear," explained AJ. "I don't want to frighten her."

"Something is wrong, isn't it?" said Emily.

"There's been a white van driving around our house," said AJ. "Have you seen it?"

"I haven't," answered Emily. "But I'll be sure and look for it if you want. Is something wrong?"

"Every time it reaches our house, it slows down," said AJ. "I tried to get the license plate number, but it was covered with mud. But I could tell that it's out of state."

"Maybe they're lost and trying to find someone's house," said Emily.

"That's what Grandma and Mom said," said AJ. "But I get the worst feeling inside when I see it. It looked like two men were inside, but I couldn't really tell through the dark windows. Don't laugh, Em, but I think they're kidnappers and they want Sara. You know how cute she is and how she always gets a lot of attention. They've probably noticed her walking home from kindergarten, and now they know where she lives."

"Is Sara with you?" Emily asked.

"She is," said AJ. "We're going to work on puzzles. I don't dare let her go outside."

"Isn't anyone else home with you?" asked Emily.

"No," answered AJ. "Mom took Grandma to the doctor. Jen and the twins are at school until late. And Dad doesn't get home until six-thirty."

"Do you want me to come over?" Emily asked.

"I think we'll be fine," said AJ. "I'm going to keep Sara in the house with me."

"If you get scared," said Emily, "call me and I'll be right over. Okay?"

"Thanks," said AJ. "I'm glad you're home. If I need you, I'll call."

When AJ hung up, she felt somewhat calmer. She was thankful she had such a good friend. She knew she could count on Emily, and that meant a lot.

Sara walked into the kitchen just as AJ hung up the phone. Her arms were loaded with boxes of puzzles.

"Should we do the one with the dogs?" Sara asked. "I love that one."

"I like that one, too," said AJ. They dumped the pieces all over the counter and proceeded to turn each piece upright.

AJ occasionally glanced out the living room window, just in case the van drove by. She hoped it wouldn't.

It was almost five-thirty and nearing time for dinner when her mother and her grandmother drove into the driveway.

"I'm so glad you're home!" exclaimed AJ when they walked into the kitchen. "Was everything all right with Grandma at the doctor's?" AJ noticed her mother's swollen eyes. "Mom, what's the matter?"

"Oh, I'm okay," said her mother, glancing at the clock. "Oh dear, it's nearly time for dinner and I've not got a thing fixed. Could you help me, AJ?"

Grandma didn't say a word, but quietly went into her room and closed the door.

"Mom, is something wrong with Grandma?" AJ asked.

"Oh, honey, it's been a long afternoon at the doctor's and Grandma's tired. She'll be fine. She just needs some rest."

AJ sensed that there was more than her mother

was telling her. She hurried and set the table while Sara continued working on her puzzle.

That night at dinner, everyone except Sara seemed extra quiet and somber, something which was rather unusual at the Bexton home. Even Jen, who was always talking, had very little to say. Jake livened up the group a little when he joked with his twin brother about baseball practice.

"One more fast ball like you threw at the coach and we'll both be ejected from the team," Jake said. "I've never seen a ball fly like that one!"

Josh's cheeks flushed a bright red. "One of the sophomores showed me how to throw a 'speed ball.' I didn't know it'd go so fast."

"What happened?" asked Dad. "Did you strike the coach out?"

"*Knocked* him out was more like it," said Jake, laughing at the top of his lungs. "Josh's ball hit him right in the thigh and it knocked him to the ground."

"Is the coach all right?" Mother asked.

"Oh, yeah, he's pretty tough," said Josh. "He said that tomorrow in practice, he's going to pitch to me."

By this time, everyone was laughing. Even Grandma.

After dinner, when Grandma and AJ were putting away the last of the dishes, Grandma turned to AJ. "Should we go sit on the porch for a little while?" she asked.

AJ was glad she didn't have any homework. She had waited for a chance to talk to Grandma. They slipped outside without anyone even noticing.

"What did the doctor tell you today?" AJ asked. "I

wanted to ask you earlier, but I could tell you didn't want to talk about it."

Grandma smiled. "You sure do know me, AJ. It seems that you can tell exactly what I'm thinking."

AJ laughed. "And you always seem to know what I'm thinking."

Her eyes met Grandma's. "Is there something you want to tell me?"

"The doctor has been taking some tests to see why I've been so tired lately," said Grandma. "Not all of the results are in yet. I guess I was upset about waiting all that time in his office and then finding out I still have more tests to take."

"Does he think there's something wrong?" AJ asked.

"When you get my age, there's always something wrong," said Grandma. "But I'm not going to dwell on it. There's too many good things in the world to think about without wasting your time on the bad. Besides, everything always works out."

AJ scooted closer to Grandma. "I know what you mean," said AJ. "When Benj left to go on his mission, I thought I could never get along without him. It was really hard. But then he started writing me letters and telling me about the people in Germany. When he told me about his first baptism, I knew everything was for the best, even though I still missed him."

"And think about how ornery your neighbor Brother Gruen was," said Grandma. "I wondered if that old man would ever be nice to you. And now he's a good friend."

"Sometimes I wish I knew how everything was

going to turn out," said AJ. "But I guess that wouldn't be too good, would it? Maybe if we saw the hard times, we'd just give up."

"You're wise beyond your years," said Grandma. "Most people take a whole lifetime to figure that out, and you're only twelve."

"I think I learned some of that from Miranda," said AJ. "When you and Miranda came to live with us, I thought everything was going to be perfect. Remember the first day when Miranda ran off? And remember how I had to sleep in the garage to keep her quiet?"

Grandma and AJ both laughed.

"You probably wished Miranda had stayed in St. George when she dug up Brother Gruen's flowers," said Grandma. "I didn't know if he was ever going to forgive the two of you."

"But look at all the good that came from that terrible incident," said AJ. "I now have a good friend, I know a lot more about flowers, and Miranda's going to obedience school."

"And Brother Gruen is going to church every Sunday," added Grandma.

"Look!" exclaimed AJ. "There's a falling star."

"That's a sign of good luck," said Grandma. "Grandpa always told me that falling stars and good luck are synonymous, and I always believed him."

"Do you miss Grandpa?" AJ asked.

"Oh, yes, I do miss him," said Grandma, her voice choking a little. "But it's a crazy thing, AJ. Even though he's dead, I still feel his presence."

AJ looked confused.

"I don't know if it's because we shared so much

or because we got along so well," Grandma said, "but it seems like he's still a part of me and close to me. Sounds funny, huh?"

"Not really," said AJ. "I think if you love someone enough, they'll always be a part of you."

Grandma reached over and put her hand on AJ's knee. "This is going to sound really crazy, but sometimes I imagine Grandpa and I greeting each other when I die."

"Oh, Grandma," gasped AJ. "How can you say that? I mean, about . . . well, you know."

"Yes, I know," said Grandma. "When Grandpa died, I never could say that word. I always told people he had passed away. So I can understand how you don't like to hear that word. But that isn't the important part. When I imagine seeing him again, I think of how happy we'll be to see each other. I have a feeling that he's missed me as much as I've missed him."

"Do you think he'll still laugh like he did when he'd tell us funny stories?" asked AJ. "I can still hear him laughing."

"Probably so," said Grandma. "And believe it or not, AJ, someday you'll grow old, and when it's your turn to leave the earth, you'll get to see Grandpa again, too."

"That is kind of a neat thought," said AJ. "I'd never really thought about it before. Maybe it's because you know you'll see Grandpa again that you always feel like he's near."

As AJ sat with her face cupped in her hands, thinking about what Grandma had said, she suddenly blinked.

"Grandma, did you see those car lights just flicker off?" she asked.

"No, honey, I wasn't noticing," said Grandma.

"Just watch down the street," said AJ. "I'm sure there's a parked car that turned off its lights, but no one got out."

Grandma stared into the darkness. Suddenly, an engine started and out of the darkness a van drove away. A white van.

AJ felt her heart begin to race.

"Grandma, it's the white van that keeps driving around here," she said.

"C'mon, AJ," said Grandma, "let's go inside. I think we need to tell your father about this."

AJ took hold of her grandmother's arm. "Grandma, would you think I'm crazy if I told you that I think they're kidnappers?"

"I don't think you're crazy, AJ," said Grandma, "although I seriously doubt they are kidnappers."

"But on television there are always stories about people taking children," said AJ. "And for some reason, ever since I first saw that van today I've had a terrible feeling that the people in it are bad—like they're out to hurt someone."

"Sometimes I think television puts too many frightening ideas into young people's heads," said Grandma. "But I do have to go along with your feelings. I'll always remember when I took your mother as a little girl to the park."

"Did someone try to kidnap her?" AJ asked.

"Oh, no, nothing like that," said Grandma. "But your mother noticed a man who kept staring at her. She was only a little girl. Finally, she came up to me and asked if we could go home because there was a mean person in the park. That was the only way she had to describe her feelings."

"So did you leave?" asked AJ.

"Oh, yes," said Grandma. "A very wise pediatrician once told me that children are blessed with intuitive feelings. He told me to trust their feelings. And so without saying a word, we left the park and that stranger. Nothing ever happened, and over time your mother quit talking about that mean person."

"Do you think he would have done anything to either of you?" AJ asked.

"I really don't know," said Grandma. "But sometimes it's better to follow those types of feelings and remove yourself from the situation, rather than take chances."

AJ nodded in agreement.

"We'd better go inside," said Grandma. "We need to talk to your father about that van. Perhaps he should call the police so they can check it out."

AJ and Grandma closed the door behind them. They didn't see the white van lurking around the corner.

3

The Open Gate

Early the next morning, AJ rushed out the door for school. She spotted Emily waiting for her on the corner.

"Hi, Em," she called. "Sorry I'm so late."

"That's okay," said Emily. "We'll still make it if we hurry."

"I had the worst time getting to sleep last night," said AJ. "All I could think about was that van. Did you ever see it?"

"I didn't," said Emily. "I told my parents to watch for it, too. But they didn't see it either."

As AJ flung her backpack over her shoulder, she glanced toward her home. "Oh, no," she moaned. "Miranda's out in the front yard. I must've left the gate open on her pen."

"Do you want to hurry back and get her?" asked Emily.

"I don't think I've got enough time," said AJ.

"And Miss Bleezer's been in such a bad mood this week that I don't want to make her mad if we're late."

Miranda ran around the yard to the garage. "I'm sure Mom will see her out and put her in her pen," said AJ. "We'd better get to school."

AJ and Emily started running. They slowed down long enough to wave to Brother Gruen. "Your flowers sure look pretty," AJ called as they raced by.

AJ and Emily burst into their classroom just before the bell rang. Miss Bleezer was at her desk. AJ thought it quite unusual that she didn't say anything about their coming in late. Miss Bleezer seemed to enjoy embarrassing AJ in front of the class. *Maybe this will turn out to be a good day after all,* thought AJ.

AJ pulled out her library book. The first fifteen minutes of every morning were spent in quiet reading while Miss Bleezer took roll. However, this morning Miss Bleezer sat stiff at her desk staring—staring at AJ.

"AJ," said Miss Bleezer quietly, "would you please come up to my desk?"

Oh, no, thought AJ. *What have I done now?* She quickly made her way up to the front of the room.

Miss Bleezer motioned for AJ to sit in a chair by her desk.

"I've been reviewing your grades, AJ," Miss Bleezer said. "And I remember how well you did in the writing contest. I think you should consider writing an essay for seventh grade honors English."

AJ gasped. "What would I have to do?"

Miss Bleezer's shoulders relaxed and a faint smile

crossed her face. "The counselor from the junior high is coming this Friday. If you can stay after school, the counselor will meet with all the eligible students. That's when you write the essay."

"When do they let me know if I make it?" asked AJ.

"They'll contact you sometime during the summer," answered Miss Bleezer. "But when you register for junior high on Friday, you will register for honors English. If you don't make it, they'll automatically put you in a regular English class."

"Is there a possibility that anyone else in our class might make honors English?" AJ asked, glancing over at Emily.

"Why don't you come right out and ask me what you want?" said Miss Bleezer. "You're almost ready to go into seventh grade. For heaven's sake, don't waste time beating around the bush! And yes! Emily is also on the honors list."

AJ grinned at Emily, who had been sitting at her desk watching them.

"Now, take your seat and catch up on your reading," said Miss Bleezer brusquely. "By the way, congratulations!"

Miss Bleezer actually smiled. *Oh, yes!* thought AJ. *This is going to be a great day!* She watched Miss Bleezer motion for Emily to go up to her desk.

The hours rushed by. AJ strugged to keep her mind on her lessons. She kept thinking about junior high. She had heard so many horror stories of going into seventh grade. The lockers get jammed. You have only five minutes to get to class. And no recess.

But if Emily and I can get into honors English, AJ thought, *then we'll have at least one class together.*

As soon as the bell rang, both Emily and AJ rushed out of the classroom.

"Won't that be great if we both get into honors English?" said Emily.

"That sure would," agreed AJ. "I hope we both do really good on the essay this Friday."

As AJ and Emily walked home, they caught sight of Brother Gruen weeding his flowers.

"Hi!" they called.

"You girls sure were in a hurry this morning," he said. "I can always tell when you two are late."

Emily and AJ laughed.

As AJ recalled hurrying to school that morning, she suddenly remembered that Miranda had been loose.

"Did you notice Miranda running around today?" AJ asked. "She was loose this morning, and I didn't have time to put her inside her pen."

"Can't say I did," said the old man. "At least I never caught her in my flower beds." He winked at AJ. Miranda had been the ruination of his flowers in the early spring.

"AJ," interrupted Emily. "Did you ever ask Brother Gruen if he saw the white van you told me about?"

AJ's eyes widened as she told her neighbor about the van in their neighborhood.

"Come to think of it," he said, rubbing his whiskery chin, "I did see a white van around here yesterday. It was going real slow and I thought the driver must be lost. I saw it circle around here a couple of times. Then I got busy and didn't notice it anymore."

"Did it have dark tinted windows in the front and no windows in the back?" asked AJ.

"I think it did," said Brother Gruen.

"That's the one!" exclaimed AJ. "Every time it drove in front of our house, it slowed down, like they were looking for someone."

"They were probably lost," mused the old man.

"Did you see Sara walking home from school earlier today?" AJ asked.

"Nope. I didn't," answered Brother Gruen. "But then I could've been in the house."

AJ panicked. "We'd better be getting home," she told her neighbor. "See you tomorrow."

"AJ," said Emily, trying to keep up with AJ's pace. "Why are you in such a hurry?"

"Em, I'm scared," said AJ. "What if those guys in the van kidnapped Sara when she was walking home from school."

Both girls were out of breath as they reached AJ's home. "Sara! Sara!" AJ called.

No answer.

AJ and Emily rushed to the back door. It was locked.

AJ fumbled nervously with the key as she opened the door. On the table was a note from her mother.

> Dear AJ,
>   I had to take Grandma to the doctor. I'm picking Sara up at school, so don't worry. We'll be back by 5:00.
>   Love,
>   Mom

AJ and Emily both breathed a sigh of relief.

"Sometimes your imagination runs away with you, AJ," grinned Emily. "I think I'd better be getting home."

"Thanks, Em," said AJ, somewhat embarrassed. "I guess I do let things get a little exaggerated sometimes."

They both laughed. "See you in the morning for school," said Emily.

AJ hoped that Jen or the twins would be coming home from school soon. She didn't like being alone in the house. She grabbed a slice of bread. *I'll see if Miranda wants out of her pen,* she thought.

"Miranda!" AJ called. "C'mon, girl."

AJ pulled open the gate to Miranda's pen. It was unlatched. No dog was in sight. AJ quickly looked inside the doghouse. No Miranda.

"Miranda!" AJ cried. "Miranda!"

4

Miranda's Disappearance

AJ's heart raced. Perhaps her mother hadn't noticed Miranda running loose. *But Miranda wouldn't run away,* thought AJ. *Something has happened to her.*

AJ ran out to the front yard. "Here, Miranda," she called. "Here, girl."

AJ spotted Brother Gruen still out working in his flower bed. "Brother Gruen," AJ called as she ran to his yard. "H-have you seen Miranda?"

AJ was out of breath and could hardly speak.

Her neighbor quickly dropped his hoe. "Well, for pete's sake," he said. "What are you all out of breath about?"

"I can't find Miranda," said AJ. "Are you sure you haven't seen her today?"

"I'm sure," said Brother Gruen. "But after you left, I thought more about that white van. I remembered that I saw it this morning. But it was pretty early. In fact, it was soon after you and Emily rushed off to school."

"That's when Miranda was out in the yard," said AJ.

AJ's dark brown eyes widened. "Do you think they could have taken Miranda?" she asked. "Maybe that's why they were always stopping in front of our place. I thought they were kidnappers. I never thought about them taking Miranda."

"Hold on just a minute," said Brother Gruen. "She's probably out chasing some cat. She'll be back. Just be a little patient."

AJ looked toward her home just as her mother drove into the driveway.

"Thanks," said AJ. "Thanks for helping me. I'm sure you're right. I'll ask Mom if she's seen Miranda."

To AJ's disappointment, neither her mother nor her grandmother had seen Miranda all day.

"I didn't notice she was loose," said her mother. "And I forgot to check on her during the day. You're always so good about feeding her in the morning and taking care of her that I completely forgot about her."

"Grandma," said AJ, "do you think there's any chance that someone could've taken Miranda?"

"She is a registered retriever," said Grandma. "More than once I had people offer lots of money for her. But I never took them seriously."

"Do you think that someone stole her so they could sell her?" asked AJ.

"It's possible," said Grandma. "But she could also be out running around the neighborhood. Let's wait for a while and see if she's back by dinner."

Sara bounded into the kitchen. "Look what Grandma's doctor gave me," she said. Sara waved a blown-up white plastic glove in the air. "This is my hand balloon."

AJ couldn't help but laugh at her little sister. She noticed Grandma turning to leave and she followed her into her bedroom.

"Grandma," said AJ. "What did the doctor find out from your tests?"

Grandma put her purse on the bureau. "There's a few little problems, but then, what can I expect at my age?" Her voice was shaky, and AJ sensed she wasn't telling her everything.

"Is it your heart or anything like that?" AJ asked, trying to get more information.

"My heart is fine," said Grandma. "It's just that my old body is giving out on me."

"What can I do to help?" asked AJ. "If you're supposed to exercise more, we can take walks every night."

Grandma's eyes were watery. "Just keep making me happy, AJ," she said. "I love when you come home from school and tell me about your friends and the things you do. I forget all about my problems when you and I are together."

"Actually, I think I give you more problems," said AJ. "If I would've locked Miranda up this morning, then she wouldn't be gone. Now I've added another problem for you to worry about."

"I'm not too worried about Miranda," said Grandma. "She's terribly smart. If she's got herself in some trouble, I have a feeling she'll find a way out. Now, let's go help your mother with dinner. Your brothers will be home soon and I have a feeling they'll be starving—as usual."

AJ put her arm around Grandma as they walked into the kitchen. She couldn't help but notice Grandma's bony shoulder. "We've got to fatten you up, Grandma," said AJ. Grandma laughed, but it wasn't the same robust laughter Grandma had when she had come to live with them a few months ago.

Long after dinner was over and the dishes were done, AJ was still watching and waiting for Miranda to return. She sat on the back porch steps anticipating a bundle of golden fur to come bouncing into her arms.

"AJ," Mother called, "you'd better come in. It's getting late and you've got school tomorrow."

AJ reluctantly left the porch. That evening it was Sara's turn to offer the family prayer. She blessed everyone in the family, and especially Benj on his mission. In closing she asked that Miranda would find her way home.

As AJ said amen to the prayer, she fought back her tears. Grandma's only request was for AJ to make her happy. She must not cry and upset Grandma.

That night, long past her usual bedtime, AJ lay awake, wondering where Miranda was and worrying about her finding her way back. Sara was sound asleep when AJ looked at the clock. 1:30 A.M. AJ had an idea. If Miranda was lost, she needed help.

AJ slipped out of bed and quietly turned on her desk lamp, hoping not to waken Sara. She closed their bedroom door, and then sat at her desk with paper and pen. If Miranda was lost, she needed to put an article in the "Lost and Found" section of the newspaper.

AJ sat straight up. *I didn't see the white van today,* she thought. *And Brother Gruen had seen it early this morning when Miranda was out in the yard. I'm sure that van has something to do with her disappearance.*

AJ quickly wrote a description of Miranda. Then she added a description of the white van. If anyone knew anything about Miranda, they were to call the Bexton home.

But I need a reward, thought AJ. *That's the only way I'll get people to read this.*

AJ opened the drawer where she kept her money. She had only thirty-six dollars, and that was to pay for the next session of Miranda's obedience school.

Oh, well, thought AJ. *I'll take care of that after I find Miranda.*

It was well past two in the morning when AJ slipped into bed. She slept soundly, knowing that she had at least done something to find her dog.

"AJ," Sara said, shaking her big sister. "You've got to get up or you'll be late for school."

AJ rubbed her eyes. How could it be morning already? She grabbed her reward notice and raced to the kitchen.

Her father was opening the door to leave for work.

"Wait, Dad," AJ cried. "Will you do something for me?"

"Looks like you'd better hurry and get ready for school," her father said. "What is it you need me to do?"

"I wrote this reward notice about Miranda," said AJ. "Would you mind taking it to the newspaper office when you go to work? And then I have a poster made up for you to run off at your office."

Her father read the article out loud. Grandma was at the kitchen counter. When AJ's father read the amount of the reward, Grandma interrupted.

"Make that reward one hundred dollars," she said. "I'll make up the difference."

"Thanks, Grandma," said AJ. "With a hundred-dollar reward, maybe more people will look for her."

"I'll change the amount of the reward and get this into the paper first thing this morning," said her father. "I'll run you off about a hundred copies of the poster. You'd better get ready for school."

"Thanks, Dad," said AJ. She gave him a quick hug and then raced to her room to dress. Sara had left a line of clothes strewn on the floor.

"Sara," AJ called, "come in here and hang up your clothes. Our room is a mess!"

"I've got to finish my pancakes," Sara called back.

There was no time to make the bed or hang up Sara's clothes. *I'll have to clean up this room when I get home,* AJ thought, flinging her backpack over her shoulders.

"Aren't you having breakfast?" her mother asked.

AJ grabbed a banana. "Sorry, Mom," said AJ. "I've got to run. Emily will be waiting." She gave her mother a quick kiss.

"Good-bye, Grandma," AJ called. "See you after school."

AJ raced up the street. Luckily, Emily was outside waiting, and the two hurried off to school.

"Miranda's gone," AJ said as they walked briskly. "Remember yesterday when she was out in the yard?"

Emily nodded.

"I think the guys in the van took her. Brother Gruen saw the white van right after we'd gone to school when she was out in the front yard. I didn't see the van yesterday after school, and Miranda's gone."

As they turned the corner, the two friends deliberated on what could have happened to Miranda. Because no sirens were blaring to catch their attention, neither one noticed the flashing lights of an ambulance as it raced to their neighborhood and stopped at AJ's home.

5

Grandma's Watch

"I've got a ton of homework," said AJ as she and Emily walked home.

"I do too," Emily said. "And don't forget, tomorrow's when we stay after school and write the essay for honors English."

"That's right!" exclaimed AJ. "With Miranda suddenly disappearing, I'd forgotten all about that."

The two friends parted at Emily's corner and AJ hurried home. As she tried to open her back door, she was puzzled to find it locked. *Mom wouldn't be taking Grandma to the doctor again today, would she?* She found the key and unlocked the door.

On the table was a note.

Dear kids,
    We had to take Grandma to the hospital.

Sara's over at the Hansens'. I'll be home as soon as I can.

Love,
Mom

AJ read the note again, searching for more information about Grandma. She heard a car outside and raced to the window. She was relieved to see her twin brothers with Jen. Before they could get out of the car, AJ ran outside waving their mother's note.

"We've got to get to the hospital," she said. "Something terrible is wrong with Grandma."

Her older brothers and sister looked at each other in alarm.

"Let's go," said Jake. "Do you know where Sara is?"

"She's at the Hansens'," said AJ. "Should we pick her up, too?"

"I don't know if they'd let her in the hospital room," said Jake. "Why don't we go first and find out what's wrong. Then we can get Sara."

AJ locked the back door, and the four hurried to the hospital. The lady at the information desk told them the floor and room number where Grandma could be found. When they entered the room, AJ was the first one to reach Grandma's side. Her father and mother were on the other side of the room. AJ could tell that her father was comforting her mother.

AJ gently took hold of her grandmother's hand. "Are you okay?" she asked.

Grandma smiled faintly. "Of course," she answered in a soft whisper. "I told you my old body was giving out on me."

AJ could tell that Grandma was trying to ease her grandchildren's fears. Jen and the twins crowded around Grandma.

"You gave us a scare," said Jake.

"I should've called you kids at school," said their mother as she and AJ's father joined the group. "But when we got Grandma here, they assured us she'd be all right. I didn't want to upset you kids when there was nothing you could do."

"Didn't you bring Sara?" AJ's father asked.

"We didn't know if they'd let her in the room," said Josh. "We thought we could pick her up as soon as we found out how Grandma is."

"Well, I'm just fine," said Grandma.

Her weak, shaky voice made AJ think otherwise.

"I'm going to check with the nurse," said AJ's father. "If they'll let Sara in the room, I'll see if we can bring some food up here and we'll still have dinner together."

AJ's mother turned her back from the family, and AJ could tell she was crying.

"Why don't you two boys come with me and we'll check on the food," said their father. "You girls keep an eye on Grandma."

Jen walked over to her mother and put her arm around her shoulders. They stood quietly talking. AJ couldn't make out what they were saying, but she knew her mother was having a hard time.

AJ sat beside Grandma. "Miranda still isn't home," said AJ. "But don't worry, Grandma. I'm going to hang reward posters everywhere in our neighborhood and in the schools. I know we'll get her back."

Grandma smiled. "If anyone can find Miranda, it's you." She closed her eyes for a few moments.

She looks so weak, so pale, thought AJ. Her thoughts flashed back to when Grandma told her, "Just do things to make me happy."

What can I do? thought AJ. *If I find Miranda, that'll make her happy. But I need to do more.*

AJ felt Grandma squeeze her hand.

"And how was school today?" she asked.

AJ remembered it as being long and tiring, but she must not share those feelings. "It was okay," said AJ. "Tomorrow Emily and I are writing our essays to see if we get into honors English. We're kind of nervous because we both want to get into that class."

"AJ," interrupted Jen, "I'm taking Mom downstairs so she can talk with the doctor a little more. I know Grandma's in good hands with you here. See you two in a little while."

AJ noticed her mother's shoulders shaking and she knew she was crying. She was glad Jen was there. Jen always knew what to do for their mother in upsetting circumstances.

"I'll take good care of Grandma," said AJ.

"AJ," said Grandma, pulling her close, "there's something I want to give you."

AJ was surprised. How could Grandma have anything for her here, in the hospital?

Grandma reached over into her purse and pulled out her watch.

"Sit down on the bed by me," said Grandma.

She showed AJ the watch. AJ had noticed it often when Grandma wore it. She thought it was an old-fashioned watch that Grandma must have bought when she was younger. It was gold with diamonds at the top and bottom. The band was made of black cloth, and the clasp was gold.

"Grandpa gave this to me many years ago," said Grandma. "It was at a time in my life when I had more problems than I knew how to handle. I was having a terrible time coping. I didn't think I could go on with life."

"Why did he give you a watch?" AJ asked.

"That's what I wondered too," said Grandma. "He took me in his arms one night and pulled out a beautiful blue velvet case. When I opened it, I saw this watch. Of course, I was surprised."

"Did he tell you why he gave it to you?"

"Grandpa explained that this watch was to remind me of all the fun and wonderful times we had shared. Of course, it made me cry. I had been so wrapped up in my problems, that I'd forgotten about anything that was good in my life."

Much to AJ's surprise, Grandma slipped the watch onto AJ's wrist and snapped the clasp.

"I want you to have this watch," said Grandma. "In sad times, like now with Miranda gone, I want you to think about the good times, not the sad. Think about all the fun you and Miranda have had together. Grandpa told me that the watch was to remind me that even bad times pass. He told me to remember the happy memories because it's those times which will help me through the hard ones."

Grandma looked into AJ's brown eyes. "Am I confusing you?"

AJ grinned. "Not at all. You always know exactly

what to do and say to make me feel better. I love this watch. But I can't take it. It belongs to you, from Grandpa."

"Please take it," said Grandma. "I know it's old-fashioned and you won't want to wear it to school. But put it somewhere special where you can see it often. Let it be your reminder of good times, just like it has been for me through the years."

AJ hugged her grandmother. "This will be my treasure," she said. "I promise to take good care of it."

Several footsteps were heard down the hall. "Dinner time," said AJ's father as he and the boys entered the room. "Sara's coming with Mom and Jen. Hope you're hungry. We've got a lot of food here."

AJ propped up Grandma's pillow so she could sit straighter.

"I even checked to see if Grandma could relinquish her hospital food and eat with us," said AJ's father. "She has the doctor's permission."

Sara, Jen, and Mom entered the room, smiling.

"Hi, Grandma," said Sara, her happy voice lifting everyone's spirits. "Isn't this fun? We're having a picnic in the hospital."

"Let's close the door," said Jake. "If the other patients get a whiff of this food, they'll all be in here."

As Jake closed the door, everyone either got a chair or sat on Grandma's bed. "Josh, would you bless the food?" Father asked.

After the blessing, sacks were opened, napkins passed around, and juice poured into plastic cups. There was chicken, hot-spiced potato wedges, tossed salad, hot rolls, fresh fruit, and chocolate-mint brownies for dessert.

"This really is a picnic," said AJ's mother. She turned to her husband. "Thanks. Thanks so much."

AJ's father acknowledged her appreciation with a wink.

"I'm going to tell my teacher that we had a picnic in the hospital," said Sara.

The Bexton family joined in a chorus of laughter. "Leave it to Sara to make us laugh," said Jen as she handed her little sister another drumstick.

This is one of those happy times I always want to remember, thought AJ, glancing at Grandma's watch.

6

AJ's Personal Goal

AJ called Emily early Friday morning before they left for school. She explained that Grandma was in the hospital.

"Could you leave for school kind of early this morning?" AJ asked.

"Sure," answered Emily. "Any reason why?"

"Dad got the reward posters copied and I wanted to leave some on doorsteps on our way to school," said AJ. "Would you mind helping me?"

"That'd be fun," said Emily. "I'll meet you in about five minutes."

AJ was glad she had a good friend like Emily. As they hurried through their neighborhood, they left a poster on nearly every doorstep. "I hope this works," said AJ. "I have a feeling that if I could find Miranda, it'd help Grandma feel a lot better."

When they arrived at Brother Gruen's house to leave a poster, he was out in the yard working in his flowers. "Good morning," AJ said, handing him the reward poster.

"One-hundred-dollar reward!" exclaimed the old man. "I'm sure you'll find Miranda if you're offering that much money. By the way, how's your grandmother?"

AJ explained how they had taken Grandma to the hospital. "Mom said that she's bringing Grandma home this afternoon," said AJ. "Would you like to come and visit her?"

"If you think it'd be okay," said Brother Gruen. "I think I've got something she'll like."

He waved good-bye to Emily and AJ as they hurried to school.

"I hope that essay after school doesn't take too long," said AJ. "I need to get home early and see how Grandma's doing."

After classes ended for the day, AJ and Emily met with the other students who were also writing essays for honors English.

"There's a lot more people here than I thought there'd be," said AJ as she glanced around at the full room.

"Forget about all of them," said Emily. "You're a good writer and you've got nothing to worry about."

AJ grinned at her best friend. "You always know what to say to make me feel better," she said. "Good luck, Em. I hope we both make it."

The students were welcomed by the junior high school counselor.

"Would you all take out sharp pencils and plenty of paper," said the counselor. "The topic of your essay is: 'One of My Personal Goals Is . . . ' I'll give you at least thirty minutes to write. If you finish early, please leave your paper on my desk and you're excused to leave. You may now begin."

AJ sat stumped. *My personal goal about what?* she thought. Should she write about what she hoped to be someday? Should she write about her goal to find Miranda? Ideas raced through her mind. She glanced at Emily, who was already busy writing.

If only I could talk to Grandma a minute, AJ thought. *She'd know what I should write about.* Suddenly AJ sat straight in her chair. Grandma. She was the answer to her dilemma.

AJ recalled the previous night at the hospital. Grandma's watch. Remembering the good times. One of AJ's personal goals was to figure out a way to let her grandmother know how much she meant to her.

When the counselor arose and announced it was time to finish the essay, AJ could hardly believe it. She was the last one to hand in her paper. Emily was waiting out in the hall.

"What'd you write about, Em?" AJ asked as they walked home.

"You're going to think this sounds really dumb," said Emily. "I wrote that my personal goal is to someday have a big family."

"That's not a dumb goal," said AJ. "It'd take a lot of thinking to plan a goal so far into the future."

"Actually, I wrote that I want to have a family with lots of kids, kind of like your family," said Emily, her cheeks flushing. "And when my parents get old, like your grandmother, I want them to come and live with us. I think it's neat the way you always have so many people at your home. When I go home, it's just me. Mom's at work. Dad's at work. I've often thought I'd like to have my grandmother staying with us. What did you write about?"

"Our minds must have been thinking about the same thing," said AJ. "I wrote about Grandma. And I got the best idea, Em. I'm going to make her a special book. It's going to have all the memories of the things we've done together. And then I'm giving it to her on her birthday next month."

"What a great idea!" exclaimed Emily. "See what I mean? You're always doing fun things with your family."

"But you only see one side of our family," said AJ. "You don't see some of the negative things, like never having a clean room. Your room is always neat and clean because you have no one to mess it up. Sara is really messy, and our room looks like a bomb exploded in it. No matter how hard I try, it's never straight. And sometimes when I'd like it to be quiet, Jake and Josh are playing their music and it's noisy. Jen gets mad at me if I even *look* at her perfume. It's not perfect. Sometimes I think it'd be rather nice to have a quiet home with a clean room."

"May I join you two?" asked Brother Gruen, interrupting the girls' conversation. He was all dressed up and carrying a huge bouquet of flowers. "These are from my garden. I thought perhaps your grandmother would enjoy them."

"She'll love them!" AJ exclaimed. "I hope she's home from the hospital."

"Would she mind if I came to visit her?" Emily asked. "I'd really like to see her, too."

"She'd love to have visitors if she's home," said AJ.

The front door was open, and AJ invited Brother Gruen and Emily inside. Grandma was sitting on the living room couch.

"Hi, Grandma," AJ called. "Look who I brought home with me."

"These are for you," said Brother Gruen, handing Grandma the flowers.

"Oh, my," said Grandma. "This is the prettiest bouquet I've ever seen. Thank you so much. And Emily. How good to see you."

"I hope you're feeling better," said Emily. "AJ said you had to go to the hospital."

"It's nothing," said Grandma, wanting to change the subject. "Can you both stay and visit for a while?"

"I'll get us something to drink," said AJ. "Does lemonade sound all right to everyone?"

AJ's mother and Sara soon joined the cheerful group. As AJ brought the drinks into the living room, she couldn't help but notice how good Grandma looked. She had color in her cheeks. And she seemed to have more energy.

AJ could hardly wait to begin her project of making a memory book for Grandma. She had so many things to write about. Luckily, she had no homework for the weekend. She planned to hand out more reward posters throughout the area. After that, she could work on the book.

After the guests had left, AJ took out the reward posters and showed them to Grandma. "I hope we'll get Miranda back," said AJ. "I don't know if I could ever forgive myself if something happened to her."

"She'll come back," said Grandma. "I know she will. By the way, how was your essay?"

"I think I did all right," answered AJ. She looked into her grandmother's pretty blue eyes. "I wrote about you."

Grandma's eyes lit with interest. "What would you write about me?"

"You'll see," said AJ. "It's kind of a surprise. And I know you'll love it."

"AJ, there's a letter for you from Benj," called her mother from the kitchen. "It's here on the counter."

AJ hurried to the kitchen. She took the letter into the living room. "Do you want to hear what Benj says?" she asked Grandma.

AJ and Grandma scooted close together as AJ read aloud. Benj began his letter by telling about a family he and his companion were teaching. The family was from Hungary and could hardly speak German. Benj told how he and his companion had found them and how they all struggled to communicate. But they succeeded! Benj said the family was going to be baptized. His letter read:

> The part which seemed to interest them the most was when we taught them the lesson on eternal families. They are very devoted to each other, and when we told them they could be together as a family for eternity, the mother cried.
>
> I have never been lonelier for you guys than the afternoon when we taught that lesson. How I missed you, AJ! I wanted to get on a plane and

come back to my family. Of course, I knew I wouldn't. I still have a lot of work to do out here. I know there must be more families who are waiting to hear how they, too, can be together forever.

I know this sounds really preachy, probably because I'm a missionary. But I want you to know how important it is that we stick together so we can be together forever. Life on earth is very short compared to eternity. Read the scriptures, pray a lot, and love each other. That's my message for this week. Preachy, huh? It's just because I love you.

Your brother,
Benj

When AJ finished reading the letter, she heard Grandma sniffing. Benj's letters always made the family shed a few tears. But this letter seemed to affect Grandma a great deal more than any of the others. Was it because she missed Benj? Or did it make Grandma think about Grandpa and how much she missed him?

"Grandma, why does Benj's letter . . . ?" AJ stopped. Something told her that it wasn't the right time to ask that question.

7

A Visit from the Police

Early Saturday morning AJ gathered her pile of reward posters. "I'll be back in a while," she told her mother. "When Grandma wakes up, tell her I'm out looking for Miranda, okay?"

Her mother smiled. "Good luck. Who knows, we might get a phone call today from someone who sees your posters."

AJ grabbed an apple and was on her way. The warm sun felt good on her face. She loved this time of year. Flowers bloomed, the lawns were emerald green, and trees and bushes were in full bud. School would soon be out. AJ walked briskly as she thought about summer vacation. Swimming. Tennis. No homework.

I'm going to start Grandma's surprise this afternoon, thought AJ. *It'll be fun to go through my picture albums and scrapbooks. I want this to be the best project I've ever done.*

AJ's thoughts were interrupted by a loud barking.

"Miranda!" AJ called excitedly. But to her dismay, a brown and white cocker ran to her. AJ knelt down to pet the wiggly dog.

"I sure wish you were Miranda," said AJ. She gave the dog one last pat and headed down the street.

It was nearly noon when AJ handed out the last poster. Her stomach growled, and she was glad to head for home. Just as she turned a corner, she caught sight of a white vehicle.

"The white van," she gasped.

AJ ran as hard as she could to catch up with the van. Nearly unable to catch her breath, she got close enough to see the license plate. It was from Montana. She read the numbers aloud.

"I've got to remember these," AJ whispered to herself. "How I wish I had a pen with me!"

"Hey, kid," yelled the driver, leaning his head out of the window. "What're ya looking at back there?"

AJ got a good look at the bedraggled driver. His black curly hair was thick and unkempt. He had dark eyes, and by the size of his arm and shoulder, he looked like a pretty large man.

"Get out of here!" he yelled. As he glared at AJ, he suddenly got a panicky look on his face, almost as if he recognized her. He jerked his arm inside the van and tore off at high speed down the street.

All the way home, AJ kept going over the numbers in her mind. As she rushed through the back door of her home, she grabbed a piece of paper and a pencil, and jotted down the number.

"Looks like you've seen a ghost," said her father,

coming in from Saturday yard work. "What's the matter?"

"Dad, you won't believe it," said AJ. "When I was coming home from passing out the reward posters, I saw the white van I told you about. I even got the license number."

She handed her father the sheet of paper. "And I even know what the driver looks like."

"We'd better call the police and give this to them. If they feel it important, they can get your description too," said her father, dialing the police station.

After AJ's father had hung up from talking with the police, he turned to AJ. "They were really interested in the license number," he said. "In fact, they also want a full description of the van and the driver. They want to talk with you, AJ, and said they'll be over in a few minutes."

AJ's heart quickened. The only encounter she'd had with the police was when they had come to her home and taken Miranda away. Her heart pounded.

"Don't be nervous," said her father, sensing AJ's anxiety. "They need more information than I could give them, and they think you can help."

When the doorbell rang, AJ was still nervous. But once she started telling the officers about the van, she forgot all about herself.

"It's a white van with dark tinted windows in the front and there's no windows in the back. It looks like a delivery truck," AJ told them.

"Is there anything else you can tell us?" one of the officers asked.

"When I first saw it, I was outside in our yard and I noticed it drive around our block a couple of times. Then it stopped right in front of our house," said AJ. "At first I thought they might be kidnappers." AJ's cheeks flushed. She scolded herself for saying that. It sounded so stupid.

But the officers weren't laughing. "They might be kidnappers," said one of them. "We're just glad you got the license number and description of the driver. This will help us a lot."

"But now I don't think they're kidnappers," said AJ. "The last time I saw them in our neighborhood was the same time my dog disappeared. My grandma says that Miranda is worth a lot of money, and I think they might have taken her."

The officers listened intently. "We've had a rash of calls lately about other animals, expensive animals, missing," said one of the officers. "Tell me about your dog."

AJ described Miranda and told him how she was a registered golden retriever. She handed the policeman one of her reward posters.

"She's really smart and my grandma thinks she can find her way back home, even if they did take her."

"Well, thanks a lot for your information," said the officer. "You've given us some good leads. As soon as we track down this license and find out who this driver is, we'll let you know. And we'll keep an eye out for your dog, too."

As the officers left, AJ's hopes grew. With the police looking for Miranda, they'd be sure to find her.

AJ turned around to see Grandma standing in the doorway. She looked pale and thin. AJ went over to her.

"Grandma, as soon as we have lunch, I think you need to get out in the warm sunshine. It's really a beautiful day outside."

Grandma managed a smile. "I don't feel much like eating," she said. "But the sunshine sounds great."

"While you sit in the sun, I've got some books for you to look at," said AJ. Ideas about Grandma's birthday gift raced through AJ's mind. If she had Grandma look at her picture album, she'd be able to see which pictures Grandma liked. That'd give her ideas about what to put in her memory book.

AJ grabbed two lawn chairs and had Grandma sit down in one. "Now, wait here. Even though you don't feel like eating, I'm still fixing you a sandwich. You're getting too skinny," AJ said. "But while you're waiting for lunch, you can look at my picture album."

She handed Grandma her album. "Let me know which pictures you like the best," said AJ as she went inside. AJ could hardly wait to go through the album with Grandma. Once she had an idea of what Grandma's favorite memories were, she could begin making Grandma's birthday present.

AJ pulled out ham, lettuce, mayonnaise, and tomatoes from the fridge. *Grandma really has lost weight,* she thought. *I've got to make sure she eats more.*

While Grandma enjoyed her sandwich, AJ kept turning the pages of her album. Picture after picture reminded Grandma of moments they had shared. AJ kept a mental notebook of the things she must write about.

"Look at this picture of Miranda," said Grandma. "Remember when you all came to St. George and you met Miranda for the first time?"

"She was just a puppy," said AJ. "I remember how you had a box for her in your kitchen."

"Right from the start I knew she was smart," said Grandma. "Not once did she mess on my floor. And from the very first day, I loved her."

Tears filled Grandma's eyes. "Oh, my, I remember going on walks to the grocery store with her. I was lonely for Grandpa, and it seemed that Miranda came to me at just the right time. She helped take away some of the emptiness I felt."

AJ looked at the empty dog run. How could she have been so careless? It was all her fault that Miranda was gone. If only she could find her.

"Look at this picture," said Grandma, breaking into AJ's thoughts. "Remember when your family came to St. George and took me home with you? I'll never forget how sad you were when we took Miranda to live with the Johnsons."

"That seems like yesterday," said AJ. "And then do you remember when Miranda came running down the road and jumped up on our Suburban?"

Both AJ and Grandma laughed as they recalled phoning the Johnsons and telling them that Miranda would not be living with them anymore.

Memory after memory floated between Grandma and AJ. Late that night, after Sara was sound asleep, AJ crawled out of bed. She quietly opened her desk drawer and took out a sheet of paper. At last everyone was asleep and she could begin her project. She wrote:

Dear Grandma,

You have given me many presents which I shall always treasure. Take for instance Grandpa's lucky suspenders. I love them very much. Another treasure is your watch. I will always take good care of it and remember what Grandpa told you. You are not just my grandma, you are my friend. It seems that you understand me when no one else can. You always change the sad times in my life to good times. You know what I think, and you know what I care about. And no matter how many mistakes I make, you always make me feel loved.

For your birthday, I made this book for you. It is full of memories that you and I have shared. I hope that when I give this to you, Miranda will be home with us.

Thank you for being my grandma. I will always love you and Grandpa very dearly.

Your granddaughter,

AJ

AJ tucked the letter into her desk drawer. *Now I can begin writing down my memories,* she thought. *Maybe I'll even add pictures from my album.*

AJ jumped as she heard someone out in the hall. She quickly turned off her light and listened.

8

Making the Memory Book

Footsteps shuffled in the hall. AJ quietly peeked through a crack in her door. "Hi, Grandma," she whispered.

"Goodness," said Grandma, a little startled. "What are you doing up at this hour?"

"I was wondering the same about you," said AJ.

"I can't sleep," said Grandma. "I thought maybe some warm milk might help."

AJ slipped into the hall. She took hold of Grandma's arm. "C'mon, I'll fix you some warm milk, even though I think it sounds disgusting."

As AJ poured the glass of milk, she thought of her letter to her grandmother. "I've already started on your birthday present," said AJ.

"My birthday? Why, that's still a month away," said Grandma.

"I know," said AJ. "But I can hardly wait. I think you're going to love what I'm giving you."

Grandma sipped the warm milk. "Mmm. This tastes good. Are you sure you don't want some?"

"No way," said AJ. "But I'm glad you like it."

"You never did tell me why you're still up," said Grandma. "I hope you're not lying awake worrying about Miranda."

"No, it's not Miranda," said AJ, "even though I am worried about what's happened to her. Actually, I was working on your birthday present. Then I heard you in the hall."

Grandma slipped the empty glass into the dishwasher. "Well, I think we'd both better try and get some sleep. C'mon, I'll tuck you in bed."

AJ smiled. She was much too old to be tucked into bed. But if Grandma wanted to tuck her in, that'd be just fine.

"Good night," said AJ as her grandmother pulled the covers up to her chin.

"Good night," said Grandma. "I'll see you first thing in the morning." As Grandma closed AJ's door, she stopped and grinned. "Good night, sleep tight. And don't let the bed bugs bite."

AJ giggled. That was what Grandpa had always said to her as he had tucked her into bed when she was just a little girl. *Another memory to write about,* thought AJ as she snuggled under her covers.

The following week of school kept AJ extra busy. But she still managed to work on Grandma's birthday present. By Friday night, she had put nearly everything together. All she needed was a book to put the pages in. As she helped her mother prepare dinner, an idea struck her.

"Mom, can I share a secret with you?" AJ asked. "It's about Grandma's birthday."

"Of course," replied her mother. "What is it?"

"I'm making Grandma a book which has lots of memories that we've shared. I'm using pictures from my album and then writing about the events."

"That's a marvelous idea," said her mother. "I know Grandma will love that present."

"But I need some help," said AJ. "I need a real pretty book to put all the pages in. Mom, you make the prettiest books out of material—and I was wondering . . ."

"Say no more," said her mother enthusiastically. "Let's go pick out some fabric right after dinner. This evening we'll get Grandma to watch a movie on TV with the family, and we'll put one together."

"Thanks, Mom," said AJ. "You always have the best ideas. Once the book is made, it'll be all ready to give to Grandma."

AJ could hardly wait for everyone to finish dinner. She helped clear the table and load the dishwasher. "Grandma, there's a good movie on TV tonight," said AJ. "Do you want to watch it? I need to go to the store with Mom."

Grandma sat down in the living room. "Not tonight, AJ," said Grandma. "I'm not feeling too well. I think I'll just go to bed and rest."

As AJ turned to leave for the fabric shop with her mother, she glanced over at Grandma. *She looks so tired,* thought AJ. She stopped and walked over to her grandmother's side. "How about if I bring you a treat home?"

Grandma smiled. "You two go to the store. I'm going to bed."

As AJ climbed in the car, she kept thinking how tired and frail Grandma looked. "Mom, is there something wrong with Grandma? I mean, why is she so sick lately? She's always going to the doctor, but she doesn't seem to get any better."

Her mother stiffened her shoulders and took a deep breath. "Grandma's old, AJ, and she's slowly wearing out. The doctors don't know what to do for her."

"But she will get better, won't she?" AJ asked. "I mean, she isn't going to . . ."

"Grandma will be fine," said her mother. "I'm glad she's got you, AJ. You're like her breath of life. She anticipates your coming home from school because you're always so happy and excited to share your day with her. And I know she'll love your birthday present. When people grow old, sometimes all they have or want are their happy memories."

It took only a few moments at the fabric store to find the perfect material for Grandma's book. When they arrived home, Grandma was sound asleep, and the rest of the family was in the family room. AJ quickly got out the glue gun and batting.

"Let me show you how to cut the material to fit your book," said her mother. "You can probably make most of this by yourself. But I'll help you."

AJ liked that about her mother. She always treated her as if she could do anything. Within an hour and a half, AJ held up the padded floral book. "Do you think Grandma will like this?"

Her mother beamed. "It looks just like her!"

AJ hurried and cleaned up the kitchen. "I'm going to put all the pages inside," she told her mother. "Then it'll be all done."

"Did I tell you there's a letter from Benj to you?" asked her mother. "It came in the mail this afternoon." She handed the letter to AJ.

"Thanks, Mom, for helping me make the book." AJ gave her mother a big hug before going into her room to fill the book.

Page after page of memories was chronologically placed inside the beautiful padded binder. As she closed it, AJ picked up Benj's letter. *I'm going to write him and tell him about Grandma's birthday gift,* she thought. She opened the envelope.

Dear AJ,

I had the strongest feeling that you needed to hear from me. When I received the news about Grandma, I had to go in a room by myself because I couldn't help but cry. She has always meant the world to us kids. I wish I could come home and see her one last time. She has probably received my letter, but I wish I could be there with her and tell her my thoughts in person.

Grandma and you have had an extra special relationship, AJ, and I know this must be very hard for you. But stay strong. Remember that we will all be together again someday.

Sometimes on my mission I feel alone and I miss the security of all of you back home. But I have learned that it doesn't matter how far away we are from each other as long as we remember that no matter what happens here on earth, we will be together again someday as an eternal family.

Won't it be exciting for Grandma and Grandpa to be together again? When you find yourself crying because you miss Grandma so much, remember how happy she must be, and that will make you feel better. Write me, AJ. How I wish I could be there.

Your brother,
Benj

AJ stared at the letter. What was Benj talking about? What did he mean about hearing the news about Grandma? Why did he mention how happy Grandma and Grandpa would be together?

Tears trickled down AJ's cheeks. Maybe Grandma wasn't going to get better.

AJ folded the letter. She heard her father calling the family together for prayer. Should she let them read Benj's letter?

It was Jake's turn to say the prayer. AJ noticed that he asked that Benj be blessed on his mission as well as everyone else in the family. "And bless Grandma," he continued. "Bless her that she won't be in a lot of pain. And bless us that we will know what to do to help her."

As Jake closed the prayer, AJ kept thinking of his words . . . "Bless us that we will know what to do to help her."

She walked into Grandma's room, where her grandmother was sleeping. "Please help me to know how to make Grandma happy," she whispered through her tears.

9

An Early Birthday Present

AJ tossed and turned in bed. Benj's letter had left an indelible imprint on her mind. It was past midnight. Finally, she crawled out of bed and turned on her desk lamp. She picked up Grandma's birthday book, which was completely done. As she sat quietly turning page after page, she thought she heard Grandma coughing. She opened her bedroom door. Grandma's light was on. Not wanting to wake the rest of the family, she silently crept to the adjacent bedroom. Grandma was sitting up in bed.

"Grandma," AJ whispered, "what are you doing up so late?"

A faint smile crossed her grandmother's face. "I can't sleep. Why don't you come in and join me?"

AJ crawled on top of the bedspread and sat next to Grandma. "I can't sleep either. Do you want something to eat?"

"I don't feel like eating right now," said Grandma. "But you go ahead and fix yourself something."

But AJ didn't feel much like eating either.

"Have you heard anything about Miranda?" Grandma asked.

AJ shook her head.

"She'll be back," Grandma said, taking hold of AJ's hand. "I'm glad we have some time together. There's something I need to tell you."

AJ's heart quickened. She thought of Benj's letter. "Before you do," AJ said quickly, "there's a surprise I have for you."

AJ slipped into her room and grabbed Grandma's birthday present.

"I know it isn't your birthday yet," she whispered as she laid the floral book on Grandma's lap. "But you know how I can't keep surprises from you. Go ahead. Open it. This is what I've been working on for your birthday."

Grandma's eyes filled with tears.

"It's a book of memories," said AJ excitedly. "We've done so many fun things together. I don't want you to ever forget them."

Grandma could hardly speak. Her frail hands trembled as she turned the pages. "Oh, my," she finally said. "You've even got some pictures of Grandpa."

"Wasn't that funny when the three of us went bowling?" AJ said. "Grandpa was going to show us how to make a strike."

"You were hardly big enough to hold the bowling ball," added Grandma.

"Remember when he took the ball and showed me which fingers to put where?" AJ started laughing as she recalled again that memorable event. "I couldn't understand what he told me, and he got a little frustrated. He poked his fingers into the holes to make me understand, and then he couldn't get them out."

By this time they were both laughing aloud. AJ put her hand over her mouth. "We've got to be quiet," she whispered. "We'll wake everybody up."

"Look at this picture," said Grandma, pointing to a photograph of AJ at the swimming pool. "How I remember your coming to St. George and wanting to live in the pool! We couldn't get you out long enough to even eat."

"Remember this, Grandma? Jen, Sara, Mom, and you and I made Easter hats. We dared each other to wear them to church on Easter Sunday."

Grandma smiled. "And there were lots of people who noticed them when we walked through the church doors."

It was half past two in the morning when they came to the last page. Grandma read AJ's letter.

"What a wonderful birthday present!" she said, reaching over and giving AJ a big hug. "You couldn't have done anything nicer."

AJ shivered. "I guess I'd better get to bed." She turned toward her grandmother. "Grandma, was there something you wanted to tell me?"

Grandma looked into AJ's eyes. "No, I think that can wait. Why don't you sleep in here with me," said Grandma. "You might wake up Sara. Besides, I really don't want to be alone."

"That's a great idea," said AJ. "Maybe we can sleep in tomorrow morning since it's Sunday."

AJ turned off the light. She snuggled under the warm covers. "Good night, Grandma," she said softly. "I sure do love you."

"Good night, AJ. I sure love you, too. And thanks for the wonderful birthday present. That made me happier than anything else you could have done."

AJ slept soundly. She abruptly awoke to the phone ringing. She heard her father answer. "Yes, this is Mr. Bexton. That's right, a golden retriever."

There was a long pause. "That's great news. We'll be waiting to hear from you."

AJ jumped out of bed. "Dad! Was that about Miranda?"

Her father grinned. "The police think they've found the man who matches your description. They're going to check it out this afternoon and let us know what they find."

AJ rushed into Grandma's room. "Did you hear that? The police think they've found the man who took Miranda. We'll be getting her back really soon."

The news was apparently good medicine for Grandma. "That's wonderful!" she exclaimed. "Oh, my, I guess I'd better get dressed, since we'll all be going to church today."

It was a sunny, warm spring Sunday as all the Bextons loaded into their Suburban and went to church. They made their usual stop at Brother Gruen's to give him a ride. He was delighted when they told him the good news about Miranda.

AJ could hardly wait to tell Emily the good news. It was hard to keep her mind on Sister Day's lesson. She kept imagining what it would be like to see Miranda.

AJ heard her Merrie Miss teacher call her name.

"Could you answer that?" Sister Day asked.

AJ felt her cheeks burning with embarrassment. "I'm sorry. I wasn't listening very well. Could you repeat the question?"

She heard some of the girls giggle.

But Sister Day didn't laugh or act the least bit irritated. "I asked if anyone had ever experienced a time when they asked Heavenly Father for help and their prayers were answered."

"I can think of a lot of times," said AJ. "But the most recent had to do with my grandmother's dog. She was stolen. I didn't know what else to do except pray for help. This morning the police called and said they've found the man who took her. I guess that's how Heavenly Father answered my prayers."

"That's a special story," said Sister Day. "I have one more question. When your dog was taken, did you only pray and do nothing else?"

"Oh, no," answered AJ. "I made up a reward notice for the newspaper and some flyers. Emily helped me deliver a lot of them. I spent one Saturday morning delivering the rest."

"Is that all you did?" Sister Day asked.

"Not quite," said AJ. "No matter where I went, I was always looking for her or for the white van the man drove. And sometimes after dinner, I'd walk around our neighborhood and call her name."

"So there was a lot more to your finding your dog than just asking Heavenly Father to do it all," said Sister Day. "This is what our lesson is on today. When we need help, we need to call upon Heavenly Father. But we also must do all that we can to help ourselves."

"But maybe the police would have found her dog without AJ going around delivering the reward posters," said one of the girls.

"Not really," said Emily. "AJ had to first get the license number of the van so she could give it to the police. If AJ hadn't done that, they wouldn't have had any leads to help find Miranda."

Sister Day continued with the lesson. AJ made sure she paid attention, even though she couldn't totally squelch her excitement about finding Miranda.

After church, AJ and her mother quickly set the

table while Jen took the roast out of the oven. Sara placed the napkins, and the twins helped fill the glasses with ice water. Dad helped Jen pour the hot drippings into a pan to make gravy.

AJ noticed Grandma go quietly into her bedroom. She followed her.

"Grandma, can I help you with anything before dinner?"

"I'm so tired," Grandma said. "I need to take a rest before I eat. Save someting for me."

"But you need some food," AJ insisted.

Her grandmother pulled down the covers and crawled into bed. "Let me rest just a little while," she said. AJ's birthday present was on her grandmother's nightstand. Grandma reached out and patted it warmly. "AJ, I sure love this book." Her weary eyes closed.

"Have a good nap," said AJ, softly kissing her grandmother on the cheek. "I sure do love you."

As AJ walked into the hall, she turned to look at Grandma. *She looks so peaceful,* AJ thought. *I hope she'll feel better after her nap.*

The family was finishing dessert when the phone rang. AJ's heart raced with anticipation that it was the police with news about Miranda. Her father answered. "Yes, this is the Bexton residence."

A frown crossed his forehead. "And what else did you find?" he asked. The concerned furrows deepened. "Thanks for calling. If you find out anything else, I'd appreciate knowing."

"Was it the police?" Jen asked. "Did they find Miranda?"

Dad sat back down at the table. "They found the

man in the white van. They also rescued several animals, which were in cages, from the back of the van. But they didn't find Miranda."

AJ fought back the tears. "Maybe they've taken her somewhere and she's hidden."

"The police said that when they questioned the driver about a golden retriever, the man said it had escaped. That was all they could get out of him."

"Don't give up," AJ's mother said, putting her arm around AJ's shoulder. "You passed out a lot of posters, and someone might recognize her and call us."

"The posters have been out for over a week," mumbled AJ. "There's no way someone's going to find her now."

"Look, AJ," said Jake, "we'll get in the car and drive around calling Miranda's name. We'll even go into Salt Lake and look for her. You can't give up now."

"Thanks, Jake," said AJ. Tears filled her eyes. "When Grandma wakes up, I guess I'd better tell her the bad news."

Quietly, everyone helped clear the dishes. AJ looked out the spacious kitchen window into the backyard. The empty dog run looked forlorn.

AJ waited alone in her room while Grandma slept. Every time she thought she heard a stir, she looked in, but Grandma was still asleep. It was late in the afternoon when her mother came into her room.

"I think we need to wake Grandma and have her eat something," she said. "Do you still want to be the one to tell her about Miranda?"

AJ nodded. "I'll go tell her now and then have her come out and eat."

AJ walked quietly into her grandmother's bedroom.

"Grandma," she whispered. "Grandma. I need to tell you something."

Grandma lay still. AJ reached over and gently took hold of her hand. A strange, cold feeling engulfed AJ. "Grandma," AJ said again. With tears running down her cheeks, AJ knelt by the bed. "Grandma, please talk to me."

10

Saying Good-bye to Grandma

AJ turned around to see her mother standing by the door, her eyes filled with tears. She joined AJ at Grandma's bedside. Neither spoke.

Sara rushed into the room. "What's the matter, Mom?" she blurted. "AJ, why are you crying?"

AJ's mother took Sara in her arms. "Grandma's passed away," she choked.

Sara was puzzled. She looked at Grandma. She looked at her mother and then at AJ. "Has she gone to heaven?"

"Yes," her mother said softly. "Grandma's gone to heaven. Why don't you get Daddy and Jen and the twins?"

AJ's emotions surged within. How could Sara take this so lightly? How could she even think about Grandma being in heaven? She didn't even cry.

AJ looked at Grandma lying quietly. How could this happen? Her mother tried to put her arm around

AJ, but AJ stood up. This was more than she could handle. She ran into her room and shut the door. She needed to be alone.

Outside her door she could hear her family gathering in Grandma's room. She wanted to join them. She wanted to feel her father's arms around her. She wanted to cry aloud and tell everyone that she didn't want Grandma to die. But she fell on her bed and buried her face in her pillow.

"AJ," said her father from outside her door. "May I come in for a minute?"

Without her saying anything, he came into her room and sat down on the bed. "I know this is hard on you. I know you didn't expect this to happen. But don't keep your feelings inside, AJ. Talk to me."

He took AJ in his arms and let her cry. As AJ sobbed, he patted her back, just like he used to when she was a little girl and she'd fallen and scraped her knee. Only this time, it would take a lot more to heal her pain than a hug and a Band-Aid.

AJ finally pulled herself together. Her family had gathered in her bedroom. Jen and the twins wiped their red, swollen eyes. Mother choked back her tears. Even Sara was sniffing.

"We never told you this was going to happen, AJ," said her mother. "But I sensed that you were beginning to wonder why Grandma was always going to the doctor."

AJ wiped her eyes. "You mean, you knew all along that Grandma wasn't going to get better?"

Her mother nodded. "Everyone knew except you and Sara."

"Why didn't you tell me? Why did you let me go on always thinking that she'd be fine?"

"You were the one who kept Grandma going," interrupted her father. "You made her happy by always being cheerful. You talked about what you two were going to do in the future. You took away her pain by telling her about your schoolwork and your projects."

"If you had known," said Jen, "I don't think you could have made her that beautiful birthday book. You would have been too sad."

"But maybe I would've told her things that I can't tell her now," cried AJ. "Maybe I would've even done more for her if I'd known."

Josh knelt down by his little sister. "I don't think so," he said. "You would have been more concerned about her leaving us than about her being here."

Jake interrupted. "I heard you and Grandma up one night. I heard you two laughing and thought how lucky she was to have you to make her laugh."

AJ wiped away her tears. "Was it because I lost Miranda that she got sick?"

"Oh, no," said her mother quickly. "Miranda had nothing to do with it. The reason Grandma came to live with us was because of her illness. She needed to be nearer the clinic."

AJ went over to her desk and picked up Benj's letter. "Benj wrote me about Grandma. I guess that was the first time I really even thought that maybe she might not get well. But when we thought we'd found Miranda, I forgot about his letter."

"We're going to call the mission home today and

see if we can talk with Benj," said AJ's father. "It'll be really hard for him to be away from all of us at this time. But I think it'd be good if he could talk to you kids for a minute and know that we're thinking of him, too."

Her father stood up. "In fact, let's call the mission home right now before we call the mortuary or anyone else."

The family gathered in the living room. AJ glanced toward her grandmother's bedroom. *This seems like a bad dream,* she thought. *I wish I could wake up right now and not have any of this happening.*

Finally, her father got through to Munich, Germany. The mission president thought it best that they call Benj and give him the message. He gave them the number of Benj's apartment.

"Hello. Is Elder Bexton there?"

AJ ran into her room and grabbed her phone. She wanted to hear her big brother.

"This is Elder Bexton," came a clear, strong voice.

"Benj, this is Dad. We're all here together and we needed to talk with you. Grandma just passed away and we wanted you to know."

AJ heard some muffled sniffs. "Hi, Benj," she said. "This is AJ."

"Are you okay? Are you going to be able to handle this?" her big brother asked. "I've sure been asking Heavenly Father to help you."

AJ fought back her tears. "I'm all right. Thanks for your letter. That really helped me."

"Hi, Benj," Jake said on another phone. By this time Mom, Dad, Jake, and AJ were all on different phones. Sara, Jen, and Josh were waiting. AJ listened as Benj talked with Jake.

"Here, Josh," she said, handing him her phone. "Benj needs to talk to you."

Once everyone had talked to Benj, Dad motioned that it was time to hang up. Each took a turn at saying good-bye.

"Bye, Benj," said AJ. "I wish you were here."

"I do too," said her big brother. "Read my letter. Remember that we'll see Grandma and Grandpa again someday. Now you and I won't have to be afraid when it's our turn. They'll be there waiting to greet us. Bye, AJ. I love you."

AJ gave the phone to her mother, who had patiently waited. As she listened to her mother and father tell Benj good-bye, she walked into her bedroom and picked up Benj's letter.

She read, ". . . I have learned that it doesn't matter how far away we are from each other as long as we remember that no matter what happens here on earth, we will be together again someday as an eternal family."

AJ looked out her window. The sun was going down. "Bye, Grandma," she whispered. "Tell Grandpa hello from me."

11

Staying Strong

AJ awoke as she heard the phone ring. "Hi, Emily," her mother said. "AJ won't be going to school today. Grandma passed away yesterday afternoon and I don't think . . ."

"Mom, I need to talk to Emily," called AJ. "I'll take the phone in here." She grabbed the phone by her bed.

"Hi, Em. Sorry I didn't call you."

"That's okay," said her best friend. "Are you going to be all right?"

"Sure," answered AJ. "In fact, I'm going to school this morning. I just need to get dressed."

"I'll wait for you," said Emily. "Hurry. I'll meet you on the corner."

AJ's mother was surprised when AJ rushed out of her room, all dressed for school.

"I didn't think you'd want to go to school today," she said. "Are you sure you want to do this?"

"I'm sure," said AJ. "You and Dad have a lot to do today, and I'd just get in the way. Besides, I don't want to get behind in school."

AJ grabbed her backpack. "Bye, Mom. I'll see you this afternoon."

AJ raced out the door and caught up with Emily at her corner. "Guess we'd better hurry."

The girls were running when they passed Brother Gruen, who was weeding his flowers. He waved to them. Suddenly, AJ stopped and ran back to her old neighbor. She didn't think she had any tears left inside her, but as soon as she came toward Brother Gruen, tears filled her eyes.

"Brother Gruen, I want you to know that my grandma passed away yesterday." AJ fought back her tears. "You've been really good to her, and I thought you'd like to know."

The old man stopped weeding and just shook his head. "I'm sorry, AJ," he finally said. "I'm really sorry."

AJ looked at him through her teary eyes. "I hope you can come to her funeral. It's going to be on Wednesday."

The two friends looked into each other's eyes. "Bye," whispered AJ.

The day dragged slowly, and AJ was glad when the last bell rang. She felt drained of all energy. But at least she didn't spend the day crying. She thought of Benj's words . . . "Stay strong."

"What day is your grandma's funeral?" Emily asked on the way home.

"It's on Wednesday," replied AJ. "Mom said there's a lot of family coming in today and tomorrow."

"I'm coming to the funeral," said Emily. "Mom said it'd be okay if I missed school."

"Thanks," said AJ. Again she felt the sting of tears.

Cars lined the street in front of her home. When she walked in the back door, she noticed that relatives and friends had invaded the house. Sandwiches and chips were on the counter. She caught sight of her mother in the living room.

"Hi, Mom. Is it all right if I go in my room and close the door?" she asked.

Her mother sensed that AJ needed privacy more than the clutter and noise of people all around. "Could you first please get Sara for me? She's over at the Hansens', and I can't get away. That'd sure help me."

"Sure," said AJ. She grabbed one of the sandwiches off the counter and gobbled down the ham and cheese. She hadn't realized how hungry she was.

As she walked to the Hansens' home, she couldn't help but recall the mornings spent walking that same street handing out reward posters and calling Miranda's name. She thought of her Merrie Miss teacher. Sister Day told her that when she needed Heavenly Father's help, if she would do her part, then he would take care of the rest.

"What more could I do?" AJ said aloud. She felt a twinge of anger at the sense of injustice she felt. Not only had Heavenly Father let her down on finding Miranda, now he had taken Grandma.

AJ quickly pushed that horrible thought out of her mind. She must not blame Heavenly Father. She felt guilty for even having those terrible thoughts.

"Hi, AJ," Sara called as she ran out of the Hansens' front door. "Are you taking me home?"

AJ grinned. Sara's cheerful greeting helped erase the previous ugly feelings.

"Let's go," said AJ. "Mom needs our help at home. There's a ton of people there."

After AJ told Mrs. Hansen thanks for keeping Sara, the sisters hurried home.

"Miranda," called Sara. "Here, Miranda. Here, girl."

"Miranda's not around here," said AJ.

"How do you know?" said Sara. "She might be trying to find us. We need to call her so she can hear our voices."

"I wish I had your faith," said AJ. "I don't think Miranda's coming back."

Sara flashed a look of disbelief. "How can you say that, AJ? Grandma said she knew Miranda would come home."

AJ knew she couldn't argue with her little sister. All the way home, she listened to Sara calling, "Here, Miranda. Come here, girl."

That evening, the Bexton home was finally quiet. The relatives had all found places to stay, and the friends had gone to their homes.

After dinner, the family gathered to discuss Grandma's funeral.

"The twins will be pallbearers," said her father. "The family wants to have some music and we thought Jen could play the harp. Does that sound okay?"

Everyone agreed.

"Since Mom has only her brother in Idaho, we thought we'd ask grandchildren from each family to speak," continued AJ's father. "Uncle Bill wants your cousin James to talk. We thought maybe AJ could say a few words from our family."

AJ gasped. "What if I start to cry?"

"I think you'd do great," said Jake. "You won't cry any more than anyone else would."

That night, AJ automatically knelt to say her prayers, but all she could do was cry. She didn't feel she could ask Heavenly Father to help her with her talk. She still felt like he had forgotten all about her.

12

A Lucky Star

"But why do we have to go to the mortuary tonight?" asked AJ. "I need to work on my talk."

"Tonight is the viewing," replied her father. "This is a time for loved ones, friends, neighbors, and relatives to come and pay last respects to Grandma."

"But I want to remember Grandma as she was in our home, not being in a casket," said AJ. "Can't I please stay home?"

"Why don't you come for a little while?" suggested Josh. "I'll bring you home early. Does that sound all right?"

AJ knew she wasn't going to get out of going to the viewing, so she agreed with Josh's idea.

The parlor was crowded. AJ kept hold of Sara's hand while her parents visited with the guests. "I want to go see Grandma," said Sara, leaning toward the casket.

AJ didn't want to go near the casket. She didn't

know if she was afraid or if she didn't want to see Grandma lying there. "Let's wait, Sara," she pleaded.

"No," said Sara, tugging at AJ. "I want to see her now."

AJ saw her mother looking at them, wondering what all the commotion was about. AJ followed Sara to the casket. Sara was fascinated. "Is Grandma really in heaven?" she asked. "Is that why she's asleep?"

"Yes, Sara," said AJ with her back to the casket. "Grandma's in heaven."

"Don't you think Grandma looks different?" Sara asked.

AJ grabbed Sara's hand. "C'mon, let's get a drink."

As AJ reached for Sara, she glanced into the casket. Grandma did look different. AJ's heart ached. She hated this. She didn't like people looking at Grandma and saying how peaceful she looked. AJ wanted to go home.

The next morning, AJ didn't go to school. The funeral was at 11:30, and the family was to be at the church at 10:00. She dreaded having to see her grandmother in the casket again.

"Hi, AJ," said James. He looked handsome in his dark suit. He'd always been one of AJ's favorite cousins, probably because they were close in age.

"Hi," returned AJ. "Have you got your talk ready for the funeral?"

"I guess," said James. "It was really hard for me to write my talk. I hope I don't get too emotional."

"I know how you feel," said AJ. "It's hard for me to even look at Grandma lying over there."

"Really?" said James. "I don't like that either. I want to remember Grandma like she was when she was alive."

At last AJ didn't feel like an outcast. James felt the same way.

All the guests were ushered out of the room. Only the family members remained. After a prayer was offered, family members made their way up to the casket. Some gave Grandma a kiss. AJ's heart raced. She loved Grandma perhaps more than anyone there. She found herself walking to the front of the room. James followed. Her heart ached within as she bent over and gave Grandma a kiss good-bye. James surprised AJ when he, too, bent over and gave Grandma a kiss. The two cousins stared at each other through teary eyes.

"Let's go into the chapel," whispered AJ's father. "It's time for the service."

AJ hurried to a corner and picked up a package, which she hugged under her arm.

AJ was determined not to cry. She bit her bottom lip and took a deep breath. Somehow she had to get through her talk.

When it was her turn, she walked to the pulpit, the package under her arm. She unwrapped the birthday present she had given Grandma. She fought back tears as she looked into the faces of her family. She spotted Emily in the crowd. Brother Gruen was sitting by her. All eyes were on AJ as she began.

"When my parents asked me to talk at Grandma's funeral today, I didn't know what I could say. Then I thought of my grandma. Whenever I think of Grandma, I feel good. She and I shared many happy times together. I hope that Grandma is watching us today, because this talk is to her. I want her to always remember the good times we've had together.

"Grandma, do you remember when I was a little girl, and you took me to the store? I took a piece of candy off the counter and hid it in my pocket. When we got to the car, you saw me take out the candy, and you asked me where I got it.

"At first I was afraid to tell you the truth. I thought you'd get mad at me. Maybe you wouldn't like me. But somehow I gathered enough courage to tell you that I took it from the store.

"Grandma, you didn't even scold me. You looked at me with your pretty blue eyes and told me that I should never take anything which isn't mine. You told me about the Ten Commandments, and one of them was that we shouldn't steal.

"You asked me how I could make the situation better. You let me decide that it was best to take the candy back and tell the clerk I was sorry.

"I've never taken anything since that day, and I doubt that I ever will, because of the lesson you taught me."

AJ continued with more of her tender memories. She became so involved in telling the stories that she forgot the audience, and for a few moments, it was like having her last conversation with Grandma.

AJ closed with the last line from Grandma's book.

Thank you for being my grandma. I will always love you and Grandpa very dearly.

Your granddaughter,

AJ

Not a dry eye could be found in the audience.

When the funeral ended, AJ crawled into the car with her family. "You sure did a great job," said Jen. All the family chimed in their agreement.

As the procession drove to the cemetery, AJ looked out the window. Kids were out in the schoolyard playing ball and chasing each other. They were giggling and laughing.

How can they be so happy when I'm so sad? thought AJ. *I wonder if there is someone else somewhere who is going to the cemetery, too, to bury someone they love.*

The dedicatory prayer was offered by Uncle Bill. AJ's father handed her a red rose to lay on the casket. And then he took the red ribbon from the flower bouquet which read "Grandma" and he handed it to AJ.

"This is your remembrance," he told her. "When you're older, you'll treasure this."

"Thanks, Dad," said AJ.

Friends and neighbors left. The family gathered at the Bexton home for a meal before they all left for their own homes.

"Why don't you come up and spend some time in Idaho this summer?" called James from the car window as his father started to drive away. "We'd have a great time."

AJ waved. "Maybe I will," she called. "Maybe I will."

AJ was tired from the long and emotional day. Yet, for the first time in days, she felt at peace. She lovingly placed Grandma's book on her shelf. She slipped the red ribbon her father had given her at the cemetery inside the book.

It was late evening when her family said prayers and they all went to bed. Even though AJ was exhausted, her eyes were wide open and her mind reeled with the happenings of the last four days.

She looked over at Sara, who was sound asleep. AJ thought how she'd probably move back to her own room where Grandma had been. But AJ was in no hurry. She needed more time for the pain to go away.

She crawled out of bed and walked quietly into the kitchen for a drink of water. She noticed the half-moon and the sprinkling of stars. The evening was warm. AJ noiselessly opened the back door and sat down on the steps. No longer was she angry. She knew Heavenly Father hadn't forgotten her. She knew he'd helped her get through her talk. "Thanks, Heavenly Father," she whispered.

As AJ looked into her backyard, she recalled how she and Grandma used to sit there and visit.

She remembered the evening when they thought a prowler was in the yard. It turned out to be their neighbor Brother Gruen. And he turned out to be their friend.

I must write Brother Gruen a letter and thank him for the beautiful flowers he sent to the funeral, AJ thought. *I know he'll miss Grandma, too.*

AJ thought about Grandma's watch, which she had placed among her keepsakes. "Remember the good times," Grandma had said.

Just then a falling star crossed the heavens. AJ smiled. She could imagine Grandma sitting there telling her, "That's a lucky star."

Quiet tears filled AJ's eyes. Suddenly, AJ felt something wet and rough on her cheek. Startled, she jumped to her feet. Standing by AJ's side with her tongue hanging out and her tail wagging was Miranda.

"Miranda!" AJ cried.

She buried her face in the dog's shaggy and tousled fur. "I can't believe it's really you!"

AJ looked into the heavens as she hugged Miranda tightly. "You were right, Grandma. You knew Miranda would come home."